DICKY-DUCK

Written and illustrated by David Wrig

Book 2: Dicky-Duck and the Mink

For Jodie

Also available in this series:

Book 1: The Hatching

Book 3: Dicky-Duck Explores

Coming Soon:

Book 4: Sports Day

Book 5: Dicky-Duck and the Kite

Book 6: The Duckling Race

Baby ducks have to be very careful, because lots of animals would like very much to eat them for breakfast. Or lunch. Or dinner. Or even as a snack between meals! Foxes, herons, buzzards, magpies and crows all fancy a nice fresh fat juicy duckling if they get the chance, but the scariest and most dangerous enemy of all is the mink. It is like a wild but extremely vicious kind of ferret, and baby ducks aren't even safe in the water because mink love to swim.

One day, Dicky-Duck had just finished off a rather large plate of baked bean sandwiches, and decided to have a nice cool swim to give the food in his rather fat belly a chance to go down. He hadn't noticed a dark furry creature slide into the pond on the far bank! He nearly wet himself when it suddenly popped out of the water right in front of him. It had fierce red eyes and sharp, wicked-looking teeth. It dived towards him with its jaws wide open, ready to snap shut like a trap!

In the blink of an eye, Dicky-Duck leapt in the air and did something we would find impossible. He paddled so hard that only his webbed feet touched the water as he ran across the surface like a water skier. He went so fast you would have thought his bottom had caught fire! It was as if he was rocket powered - and judging by the size of the baked bean sandwich he had just eaten - he probably was!

The mink gave chase as fast as he could, but was no match for a baby duck in turbodrive. He rushed headlong into Dicky-Duck's exhaust fumes, and the smell forced him to dive under water to avoid throwing up! In the meantime, Dicky-Duck was up the bank and across the lawn before the mink had got half way across the pond. Quacking at the top of his voice, Dicky-Duck charged into the house to get help.

At the very moment that Dicky-Duck shot around the corner into the house, Deefer dog was coming out to see what all the fuss was about. Dicky-Duck ran headlong into her and bounced into the air in a flurry of feathers. Deefer was so surprised she sat down with a splat - straight in her water bowl! While Deefer shook the feathers out of her eyes and the water out of her bottom, Dicky-Duck hopped on her back and shouted in her ear that a mink was in the garden.

Now Deefer is a lovely quiet and placid dog who wouldn't harm a fly, but if there was one animal that was guaranteed to make her go bananas, it was a mink! Deefer shot out of the house so fast there were sparks flying off her claws - and if Dicky-Duck hadn't managed to tuck his big webbed feet under her collar, he would have been thrown off her back.

Hanging on as tightly as he could, Dicky-Duck leaned forward and pointed to where the mink had been. Deefer whizzed around the corner of the cottage at top speed, just as the mink came speeding around from the other direction. The mink suddenly realised that its breakfast had turned into a great hairy monster with the most enormous teeth it had ever seen! It back-pedalled as fast as it could, its feet skidding as it frantically tried to avoid disaster.

Deefer was now travelling so fast, she couldn't have stopped if she had wanted to, and the animals collided head on - CRASH! Dicky-Duck shot forward like an arrow from a bow, and landed in the middle of the lawn. The mink managed to turn and run, but as it ran off Deefer's teeth clamped down hard on its tail with a snap. The mink finally wriggled free, but as it ran across the lawn it didn't notice the foot that Dicky-Duck stuck out as it went past.

The mink did a double somersault and landed with a loud splat in something squidgy and very smelly! In a flash, Deefer leapt after the mink, but it dodged to one side and darted under her legs. It fled across the garden and jumped onto the fence. It had managed to escape, and, feeling rather pleased with itself, put its tongue out at Deefer and Dicky-Duck before turning and diving off the fence.

What the mink didn't realise was that Scat the cat was waiting for him on the other side! Scat was just about the best hunter in the neighbourhood, and no mink was going to trespass on his patch! As quick as lightning, Scat pounced on the mink like a tiger. You should have heard the commotion that came from behind the fence as the mink was finally taught its lesson!

Dicky-Duck picked up his cap, then jumped onto Deefer's back as she trotted across to look over the fence and see what was going on. They were just in time to see the terrified mink running for its life. It was covered in scratches and bites, had lost one ear, half of its tail and most of its fur. What fur it did have left was plastered with seriously smelly squidge, which wasn't going to be very nice to clean off!!

"I don't think he'll be back again in a hurry", laughed Dicky-Duck!

All of the baby ducklings who lived in the garden came over to thank Deefer, Scat and Dicky-Duck for getting rid of the mink. Dicky-Duck said that Deefer and Scat were the real heroes, but Deefer lifted him up on her back and said that he was a hero too. Dicky-Duck was so pleased, he even offered to share his next baked bean sandwich with her!

EDUCATIONAL NOTE

The Dicky-Duck series of children's books are ideally suited for National Curriculum Key Stages 1 and 2. The books can be accessed and enjoyed in a variety of ways by the Primary School age range, and being both funny and highly motivational, they are particularly valuable for children beginning to read independently or simply to be read to them for fun. Children especially love the pictures, which encourage lots of stimulating discussion, and parents and carers alike will enjoy sharing many aspects of these immensely popular stories. Humour is now recognised as one of the most significant boosts to learning - especially reading - and Dicky-Duck provides a powerful and stress free way to encourage reading development.

LITERACY HOUR PRESENTATION MATERIAL

All of the Dicky-Duck series of books are available in either A3 or A4 format, loose leaf bound for 'flip chart' presentation or on overhead projector viewfoils for use in the recently introduced 'Literacy Hour' for schools. Packs of worksheets are also available which set out structured tasks designed to cover a wide ability range whilst dealing with the specific educational attainment requirements demanded by the Literacy Hour programme. Details available on request from:

LTL Publishing
Tel (01460) 64752
Fax (01460) 65957

About the Author....

David Wright started telling Dicky-Duck stories to his two young children at bedtime, and realised that by far the most successful were those which made them laugh. Encouraged by their enthusiasm, he began to write down the best ones and illustrated them as a hobby.

When David's wife read the books to children of all ages at local Primary schools where she was teaching, their response was incredible. Even the naughtiest children were captivated by the stories and pictures, and you could hear a pin drop in the classroom whenever they were read!

Constant demand from children who wanted to buy the books convinced David it was worthwhile getting them published. This is the result, which is dedicated to all those children with grateful thanks for their positive and enthusiastic support.